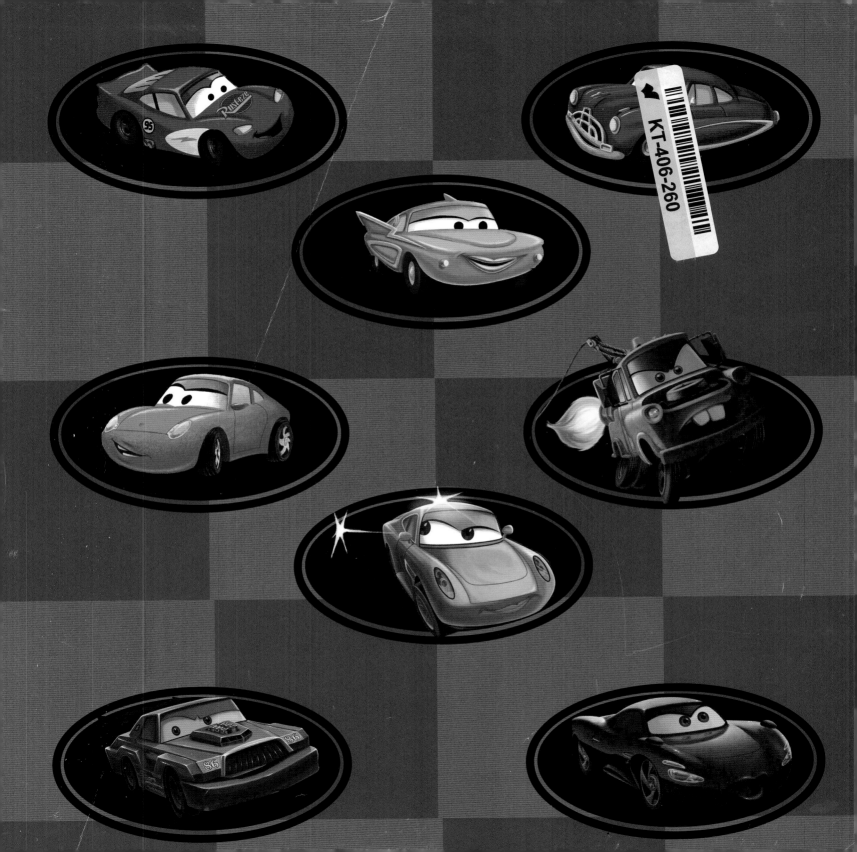

First published by Parragon in 2011

Parragon
Queen Street House
4 Queen Street
Bath BA1 1HE, UK

DISNEY · PIXAR

Storybook Collection

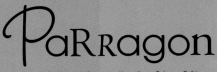

Bath · New York · Singapore · Hong Kong · Cologne · Delhi
Melbourne · Amsterdam · Johannesburg · Auckland · Shenzhen

This book belongs to:

....

CONTENTS

 Lightning's First Piston Cup   11

 Crash Course   35

 Dust up in the Desert   59

 Fame in the fast lane   83

 Rammin Relay   107

 *Cars 2* - Story of the Film   131

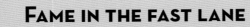

Lightning's First Piston Cup

"Pit stop! Pit stop!" cried Guido as he zoomed over and joined the gang at Flo's café. The little forklift buzzed with excitement. Would his friend Lightning McQueen win the Piston Cup?

Earlier that week, Lightning had accidentally found himself in Radiator Springs on his way to the tie-breaker race in California. He had to work hard in Radiator Springs, but he also made lots of friends. Now, everyone in Radiator Springs was sad that Lightning was gone... but also excited about his big race.

"Do you think he can beat Chick Hicks?" wondered Sally. "I hear Chick is one mean racecar."

"Lightning can beat anybody, I know it!" said Mater. Lightning and Mater had become best friends in a very short time. Mater believed in Lightning, one hundred percent!

14

15

They watched a car with a bright green paint job fill the TV screen. It was Lightning's rival, Chick Hicks!

"Lightning? Why should I worry about him?" Chick's voice came through the TV speaker. "He ended up in some rusty little town, playing with tractors and taking Sunday drives. He's not serious about winning. But I am!"

Everybody knew Chick Hicks never played fair. In fact, he caused bad accidents. In his garage, Doc saw a glint of gold through the dust and clutter. It was one of his Piston Cup trophies, the last one he earned before a devastating crash ended his racing career. He realized that he didn't want an accident like that to happen to anybody.

"Lightning's not really such a bad guy," he thought. "He just needs a good team behind him, especially if he's going to avoid Chick's dirty tricks."

Yes, Lightning needed a team, whether he knew it or not.

CRASH!

"Listen up, everybody," Doc's voice boomed down the main street from Flo's all the way to Sally's motel. "The rookie needs our help. He's out there with no pit crew and two tough opponents. I'm not going to let Lightning McQueen lose just because he thinks he can do it all on his own. Who's with me?"

Everybody was, of course! Luigi and Guido got to work choosing some tyres. Lightning McQueen would need some good ones.

By morning the crew was inside the stadium. What a feeling it was, to be surrounded by all that excitement! But the Radiator Springs crew had a job to do.

"Pit stop!" said Guido when he saw all the pitties and their tool racks. As soon as Mater unhooked him, he rolled over to a spot to set up. Sarge took command when he saw the orderly layout of the pit lane and the precise actions of the racing teams.

"You, Flo, over here," he ordered. "Guido, we need the tyres right there."

Ramone had something else in mind, "Hey, Doc! Let me give you a paint job. You gotta let these folks know that you're an important car".

"Not me," said Doc. "Try snazzing-up this pit instead. We need to show off our star car, not me."

Doc drove over to
the other side of the track to check out the
other crews. But as he neared Chick Hicks' tent he overheard something bad – really bad.
  "I'm not gonna let anyone get in the way of me winning that race today," Chick said
to his crew. "If I have to, I'll make The King and that rookie wipe out so fast their tyres
won't even spin."

Doc peeked in and saw Chick wink to his crew. "The Cup is mine, boys," said Chick. Doc felt his oil heat up. He couldn't stand for this! It was time to help Lightning, even if it took his last drop of fuel. Could he find Lightning in time to warn him about Chick's evil plans? Doc returned so fast to the group that he almost overheated!

"This is what friendship is all about," thought Doc as Ramone finished painting him. "We are all a family."

And then, as a high-octane boost rushed through him, he climbed the crew-chief platform – with Ramone's blazing letters freshly painted on his side: *Number 51, The Fabulous Hudson Hornet.*

"Look, it's the Hudson Hornet!" cried a car in the stands. The crowd roared and cheered, louder and louder. Everywhere, Doc saw a sea of flashing headlights and flying antenna balls. They were cheering for him!

Doc was too focused on the upcoming race to smile. But it was clear – Doc Hudson was proud to be back, and it felt good to hear the crowds roaring their approval.

30

It was all so exciting that no one in the crowd really cared when Chick Hicks was announced the winner of the tiebreaker race. Instead, they cheered for Lightning as he helped The King cross the finish line. They cheered as they watched Lightning cruise on over to his crew chief, Doc, the Hudson Hornet.

Yes, indeed, the crowd cheered for the real winners of this race: Lightning McQueen and his Radiator Springs family.

Back in Radiator Springs, everybody gathered at Flo's to hear about the race.
"Doc and I want to build a racing headquarters near
the town," Lightning told Sally.

Flo's V8 Cafe

Radiator Springs
New Headquarters of
Lightning McQueen 95

RADIATOR SPRINGS
RACING STADIUM

RUST-EZE
95

Doc nodded. "It will be a special design – a first-class track that won't spoil our beautiful desert landscape."

"A great idea," said Sally. "And it will put Radiator Springs back on the map."

It wasn't long before Radiator Springs became an international racing sensation. Doc and Lightning sent invitations to race cars all over the world. They came to the town to share tips and techniques on how to become better racers.

The End

CRASH COURSE

Vroom! Lightning McQueen zoomed around Radiator Springs Speedway, the town's fancy new racetrack.

Lightning spent most of his days teaching at the newly opened Fabulous Hudson Hornet Academy. But in between classes, Lightning loved driving laps especially with all his new upgrades.

"Is that the best you can do, kid?" asked Doc Hudson.

Before Lightning could answer, Mater pulled up from behind. He was gleefully driving backwards. "Better watch out! I'm right on yer tail!" he yelled.

Lightning laughed. "Well, that's my cue. Gotta go!" Lightning floored the gas and a second later he was a red streak down the racetrack.

"That's my boy," Doc said proudly.

Not far away, the Chick Hicks Racing Academy was also popular... with cars who were sly and sneaky!

Chick, who had some upgrades of his own, liked to show off in front of his students. He dazzled them with his special style of racing, also known as "The Three Cs" – cheat, cheat, and cheat.

When a sleek and devious steel-gray car named Switcher enrolled, Chick knew instantly that the new car would be a great asset to his school. So Chick taught Switcher everything he knew.

Both racing academies wanted to prove they were the best. So everyone was excited when the Race-O-Rama competition was announced. It was a special contest, consisting of four races in four different locations. Each race would pit racers from one school against the other. The winner would receive the prestigious Silver Tailfin Trophy.

"This will be great publicity for the school," said Doc.

"Especially when we beat Chick," Lightning added. It was no secret that he didn't like Chick. Not many cars did!

The first race was a head-to-head battle, two cars versus two cars. And when Chick learned that Lightning and Mater would be a team, Chick couldn't wait to sign up with Switcher.

"They don't have a chance! I'll show them who has the better school," Chick vowed.

Chick wanted to make sure he'd race to victory. So he got a bigger engine – to match his massive mean streak.

He also trained Switcher daily, making sure his star student was in prime shape to be his partner in the race.

"You call that speed?" Chick called out. "My Grandma Hicks can drive faster than you!"

Switcher narrowed his eyes and accelerated, hitting 150 mph in no time.

Chick nodded. "That's more like it."

The day of the race finally arrived. Excitement filled the air at Radiator Springs Speedway, and the stands were bumper to bumper with screaming fans.

Mater, Lightning, Chick and Switcher approached the starting line. Switcher looked over at Lightning and Mater. "That's our competition?" he said loudly to Chick. "I could beat them with my eyes closed."

"Oh, you'll have your eyes closed, because you'll be crying when I leave you in the dust!" said Lightning. ***"Ka-chow!"***

Before Switcher could respond, the green flag waved and the race began! All four cars took off to start their 100 laps.

Lightning immediately took the lead, but Switcher and Chick were right on his bumper. In fact, Chick rammed right into the back of Lightning!

"Get out of my way," Chick growled.

"Gladly," replied Lightning, smiling. Firing up his new turbo boost, he whooshed ahead.

Chick snarled. "Go get him!" he told Switcher.

Switcher grinned wickedly. "With pleasure."

With Switcher's own turbo boost, he caught up to Lightning within seconds.

"What took you so long?" Lightning joked.

But Switcher wasn't in the mood to laugh. He was, however, in the mood to cheat. Pulling ahead of Lightning, Switcher released a stream of oil behind him.

Lightning's tires skidded through the oil. He slid uncontrollably down the racetrack and was forced to slam on his brakes.

Chick pulled alongside Switcher.

"Did you see that?" Switcher boasted. "No one can stop me. See you at the finish line!" He sped ahead of Chick.

Chick's eyes narrowed. He'd had enough of Switcher's superior attitude. "If that tin can thinks he's taking first place, he's in for a surprise."

BAM! Chick rammed right into Switcher. "It's time you learned your place," he said.

Switcher flipped over and over across the track. He finally came to a stop in the infield, smoke pouring from his hood.

"I'm on YOUR team!" he yelled.

"Not any more!" Chick replied, as he accelerated.

Lightning looked on in shock. He radioed in to Doc and got help for Switcher.

Lightning and Mater pulled into the pit area.

"Pit stop!" said Guido, as he, Sarge and Luigi changed tyres and filled the cars up with gas.

"I can't believe Chick did that to his own teammate," Lightning said. "I think it's time to give him a taste of his own fuel."

"You mean like Chick's Three Cs?" said Doc. "No, I think it's time to put our own Plan C into action."

"What's Plan C?" asked Mater.

"No time to explain," said Doc. "Just follow my instructions."

After the pit stop, the cars roared back onto the track. There were only five laps left. Immediately, Doc instructed Mater to put Plan C into action.

Mater began weaving back and forth in front of Chick. Every time Chick tried to get ahead, Mater blocked his path.

"Stop it, you hunk of junk!" Chick yelled.

"Aw, shucks, flattery will get you nowhere," said Mater with a smile.

Doc then instructed Lightning to move forwards on the inside track. Lightning raced across the finish line!

"NOOOO!" yelled Chick.

On the award podium, Doc congratulated Lightning and Mater on winning the Silver Tailfin Trophy. "Great job, team," said Doc. "Plan C worked really well."

"What's the C stand for?" asked Mater.

"Cooperation," Doc explained. "Fancy gadgets and upgrades are great, but they can't compete against good old cooperation."

Lightning grinned. "And it's certainly better than Chick's Three Cs!" Doc, Mater and Lightning smiled for the cameras. Their first Race-O-Rama win felt great!

The End

Dust-up in the Desert

El Machismo raced across the dry lakebed in the canyon. The rocks he went over didn't bother him at all. This is what he was used to. This is what he was built for.

"Oh, yeeeeaaaaah!" the truck yelled gleefully, enjoying every bump and bounce. Watching from above, Chick Hicks kept a close eye on his prized student. A sly smile crossed Chick's bumper.

"El Machismo is going to crush Lightning McQueen at Autovia. Ha, ha!"

Autovia was a super-tough desert track, the next destination in the Race-O-Rama racing series. The event would be a relay race with two cars from each rival school: the Fabulous Hudson Hornet Academy and the Chick Hicks Racing Academy. The race was just a few days away and Doc still needed to find a teammate for Lightning. However, none of his students had experience with harsh terrain. Sarge wasn't a student, but he stopped by to watch his friends practice. "Don't you know how to hill climb?" he yelled. "What if you get stuck in a silt bed?"

Lightning pulled alongside the 4 x 4. "Hey Sarge, if you know so much about desert terrain, why don't you race with me?"

Sarge was stunned. "Uh…I've never raced before."

"How about I teach you how to race, and you teach me all about driving off-road?" suggested Lightning.

"All right, soldier. That sounds like a plan," said Sarge. "But kiss the racetrack goodbye. When I'm finished with you, you'll have dirt in places you didn't know you had!"

Training started at dawn the next morning, in a nearby canyon.
"Drop and give me 25 miles! Go!" Sarge barked.

Doing 25 miles was no problem for Lightning. Doing it on rocky terrain was a different story. "Ow, ow, ow!" he said as he bumped along.

"You need better tyres, soldier!" yelled Sarge. "This isn't a stadium!"

Lightning taught Sarge that racing against Chick Hicks took some special manoeuvres. "Chick Hicks doesn't play fair, so the plan is to be prepared for the unexpected," said Lightning. He put Sarge through an obstacle course full of surprises.

Sarge saved the most important lesson for last. "To win this race, you have to know how to handle one thing: silt."

Lightning frowned. "Silt? You mean the dusty dirt in old lakebeds? That's the big, important lesson?"

Sarge looked at Lightning, deadly serious. "Listen up, soldier. Make sure you're in the lead before the course goes into the silt beds. Then keep pushing the gas. If you don't, you'll get stuck. It's impossible to see through, and you'll want to stop. Don't. Just keep going."

"Yes, sir!" Lightning replied.

Race day finally arrived. The two teams rolled into Autovia amid cheers and boos. Both Lightning and Chick had new modifications, including fog lights and all-terrain tyres.

"Bow down to the tower of power! Oh, yeeeeaaaaah!" El Machismo called to the crowd.

"I think it's time that oversized heap of metal learned how to lose gracefully," said Sarge.

Sarge and Chick would be racing first. They rolled forwards to the starting line.

"Get ready to lose, old man," Chick said to Sarge, gunning his motor.

"Get ready to wave your white flag of surrender!" replied Sarge, narrowing his eyes.

Soon the green flag waved, and the race began!

71

About a quarter of the way through the race, Chick sped in front of Sarge and released a bunch of bolts on the ground behind him. It was one of his favourite nasty tricks.

But Sarge remembered what Lightning had taught him. He veered off the path to avoid the bolts and swiftly handled the rocky terrain. Then he headed to the pit stop.

Meanwhile, Chick was too busy looking at what Sarge was doing. **CRASH!**

Chick collided with a giant cactus! Ouch.

Covered with needles, Chick limped to the pit stop where El Machismo was waiting. "You make sure you beat that Lightning McQueen," Chick said sternly. "We can't lose this race."

"No problem," said El Machismo. "Wait till I get him on the dirt. I'll shred him like paper!"

Chick was pleased. But just in case, he had a back-up plan.

To guarantee Lightning wouldn't even finish the race, Chick planned to move the course marker. Lightning would be headed off-course without even knowing it!

El Machismo and Lightning both roared onto the course for the final leg of the race. Both cars zoomed across the desert plains, around tight corners, and over a rickety bridge.

When El Machismo jumped a hill, there was so much space between him and the ground that it looked like he was flying.

Uh-oh, thought Lightning. *This guy is tougher than I thought.*

Lightning remembered that he needed to be in front before he hit the silt beds. So, just as the path narrowed, he pulled into the lead.

When he reached the silt beds, clouds of dusty sand exploded all around him. He was just about to slow down when he remembered what Sarge had told him. Lightning kept moving forwards and pushed through the heavy silt. He couldn't see a thing, but he didn't dare stop. After one last push, Lightning finally made it out.

"Now that's what I call off-road racing!" he exclaimed.

All the dust from the silt beds rained down on Chick, who was hiding behind a large rock near the silt beds. Chick was blinded by the dust, but he heard a car race by. He used his windshield wipers to clear his view and then hurried to move the course marker before the next car came through.

"This will teach that hotshot to mess with Chick Hicks," he said. "Let's see how he likes a detour!"

FINISH

At the same time, Lightning glanced to the side and was surprised that El Machismo wasn't there. In fact, the truck was nowhere in sight! Lightning, however, did see the finish line in front of him. He crossed it with no problem. ***"Ka-chow!"***

"Wait!" yelled Chick. "You were supposed to take the detour!" The race officials didn't like the sound of that and took Chick in for questioning.

Lightning and Sarge were awarded the Silver Tailfin Trophy.
"Congratulations on winning your first race," Lightning said to Sarge.
"Thanks, soldier. We make a pretty good team!" Sarge replied.
Meanwhile, El Machismo had finally found his way back to the finish line. "What? I lost?" he yelled. "Oh, noooooooo!!!"

The End

Fame in the Fast Lane

"I could get used to this!" declared Lightning McQueen. He and Sally had just arrived in sunny Santa Carburera for the latest event in the Race-O-Rama series.

"Why don't we check out some of the hot spots?" suggested Lightning. He was looking very cool in his sleek new racing modifications.

"Right now you need to focus on winning tomorrow's race!" replied Sally.

Lightning was going to represent the Fabulous Hudson Hornet Academy in the upcoming race. He'd be up against a student from Chick Hick's rival racing school – but so far Chick was keeping the car's identity top secret.

"Don't worry," said Lightning as he and Sally arrived at the racetrack. "Whoever my opponent is, he doesn't stand a chance."

"Better make that she," Sally replied.

At that very moment, Chick was cruising toward them with a gleaming pink car by his side!

Suddenly, fans appeared out of nowhere and surrounded the pink car.

"Meet Candice – racing's hottest new celebrity," said Chick. Lightning was speechless. He had been gearing up to race against a mean muscle car or a rough and tough truck. A shiny pink car was the last thing he expected.

"No need to say a word," said Candice. "Fans often get tongue-tied around me. Now if you'll excuse me, I have a photo shoot!"

"What a show-off!" cried Sally.

"I've seen her kind before," Lightning replied. "You know, the type of cars who want the glory with none of the hard work."

"Speaking of hard work," Sally said, "you should have started practising by now. No more talking! Let's get moving!"

"Yes, ma'am!" replied Lightning – as he burst out laughing.

"What?" Sally asked.

"I think you've been hanging around Sarge too long!" Lightning replied.

Later, after Lightning was asleep, Sally cruised the race grounds. When she got to Candice's tent, she saw a lively party taking place inside. Candice was busy posing for pictures and signing autographs.

"Are you sure you're ready for the race?" Sally overheard Chick ask.

"Of course," Candice snapped. "I've got a few tricks even you haven't seen yet. No one is going to upstage me tomorrow, especially Lightning McQueen!"

The next morning, Sally joined Lightning while he did some practise turns.

"Just ease into it and let yourself drift," Sally suggested. Soon Lightning was turning like an expert – but Sally looked concerned.

"What's the matter?" he asked. Then Sally told him what Candice had said the night before.

"If she has to resort to tricks, then I guess she doesn't have that much confidence in her skills," Lightning declared. "Fortunately, I have plenty in mine."

When Lightning pulled up to the start line, Candice was posing for the cameras.

"Lightning, please!" she said. "You're blocking my good side!"

"You know, Candice," replied Lightning. "Doc Hudson taught me there's a lot more to racing than fame."

"Like what?" Candice asked.

"Well, things like skill, teamwork, sportsmanship..." Lightning began.

But Candice wasn't listening. She was too busy soaking up the limelight!

The starting flag went down, and Lightning and Candice sped off. Lightning quickly took the lead – and that got Candice fuming! At the first turn, she used a drifting manoeuvre that allowed her to coast right in front of him. Then, when Lightning tried to pass her, she tilted her body towards the sun. The sunlight reflected off her ultra-shiny paint and into Lightning's eyes. Now he couldn't see where he was going, and he drove right off the track!

Lightning soon rejoined the race and tried to overtake Candice, but she pushed him onto the shoulder. The next time he came up beside her, she used the sun to blind him again.

Watching from the sidelines, Sally knew she had to do something.

"Lightning!" she called. "Hang back so Candice thinks she's won for sure, then zoom up and use the drifting move we practised this morning. Once you're out in front, floor it to the finish line!"

Lightning took Sally's advice – and the lead!

"Hey, Candice!" Chick Hicks screamed. "Losers don't make the front page! I don't care how you do it, but you'd better win this thing!"

Candice sped ahead of Lightning, then swerved over to some dunes and spewed sand at Lightning as he passed her.

"This better be worth it!" whined Candice."I hate getting sand in my tyres!"

While Lightning stopped to clear the sand from his eyes, Candice smiled. Her trick had worked!

"Hey, Candice! How about looking this way?" shouted a photographer.

Candice turned, triggering a dozen cameras at once.

FLASH!

Candice blinked frantically, trying to recover from the blinding flashes.

At the same moment, Lightning raced ahead and crossed the finish line!

"And Lightning McQueen wins it!" shouted the announcer.

"I don't believe it!" wailed Chick Hicks. "How could this happen?"

FINISH

FRESH CAR

RACE

OIL

95

Lightning proudly received his Silver Tailfin Trophy. "Ka-chow!" he said as he smiled for the cameras.

Then it was time to sightsee and have some fun. Being in the spotlight was fine, but being with Sally was even better!

The End

Rammin' Slammin' Relay

"Whoa! Flashy!" Ramone exclaimed, looking at the bright neon lights of Motoropolis City.

"This place is amazing," his friend Lightning McQueen said. Lightning was looking very cool in his new racing upgrades. "I love the challenge of racing in a city. I just know we can win this!"

That night, the pair was representing the Fabulous Hudson Hornet Academy in a relay race. They were going up against Chick Hicks and a student from his racing school named Stinger.

STINGER
MOTOROPOLIS
RELAY
RACE
SATURDAY

RAMONE
MOTOROPOLIS
RELAY
RACE
SATURDAY

McQueen
MOTOROPOLIS
RELAY
RACE
SATURDAY

SLICK
MOTOROPOLIS
RELAY
RACE
SATURDAY

"I know what will help us win," said Ramone. He took Lightning to a body shop he had set up in a tent. "Check it out! A glow-in-the-dark paint job! Decked out in this, we'll really be able to see tonight."

Lightning knew there were lights all over the city to show them the way. But he didn't want to dampen Ramone's enthusiasm. "Okay," Lightning said. Paint me up, Ramone!"

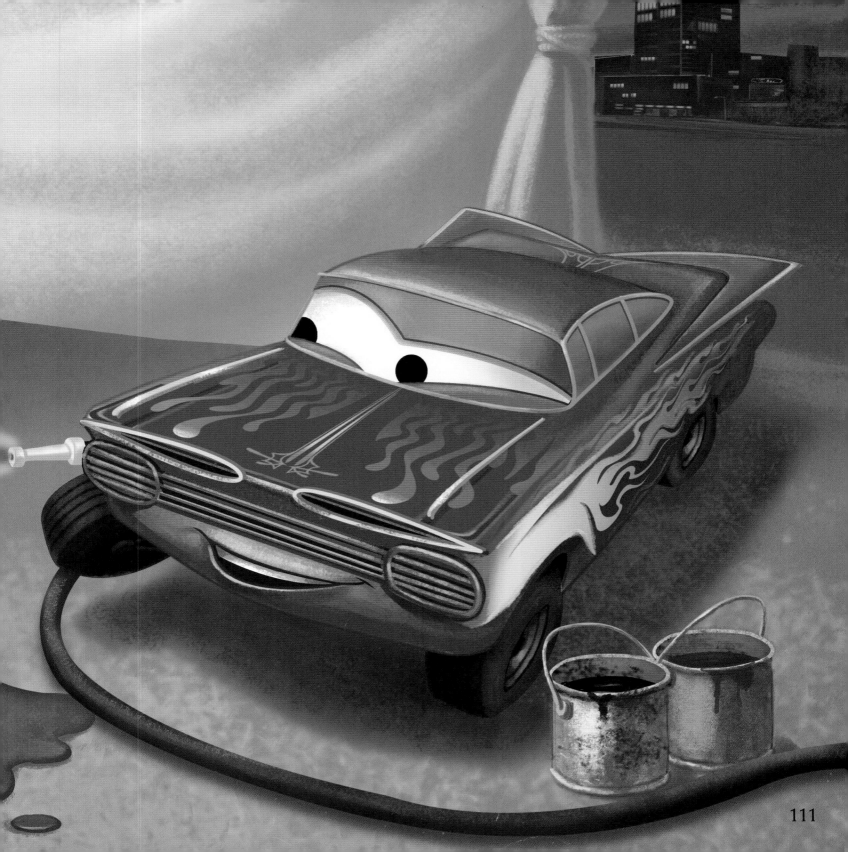

Meanwhile, Chick Hicks was working on his team's strategy. They were going to cheat – but he warned Stinger not to let the judges catch them or they'd be disqualified.

"And I don't want you to take Lightning out of just this race," Chick barked as Stinger practised his famous ramming move. "I want you to take him out for good!"

That night, the air at Motoropolis was filled with excitement.

"Welcome to another exciting event in the Race-O-Rama series," boomed the announcer. He introduced Lightning and Ramone, and the crowd went wild.

"And from the Chick Hicks Racing Academy," he continued, "Chick Hicks and Stinger!"

Chick greeted his fans, but Stinger just scowled.

"He might not talk much, but Stinger's skills on the track speak loud and clear!" Chick declared.

Ramone and Chick cruised to the starting line for the first leg of the relay. When they reached Brakeaway Tunnel, they would tag their partners. Then Lightning and Stinger would race the second leg to the finish line.

An official waved the starting flag. They were off! Chick immediately crowded Ramone towards a building. But Ramone used his super hydraulics to lift himself high above the race car. Chick slid underneath Ramone and – **SMASH!** – hit the brick himself!

Ramone took the lead, but Stinger suddenly appeared and dumped a load of bolts in the road. He wasn't even supposed to be in the race yet!

Four flats, coming up, Chick thought to himself. But Ramone's heavy-duty tyres sailed right over the mess. Chick wasn't so lucky.

"I've got to make a pit stop," Chick told Stinger angrily.
"Do whatever it takes to slow him down!"
    A little while later, Ramone saw a roadblock ahead and
screeched to a stop. Stinger had struck again!

Ramone had no choice but to detour off into a maze of one-way streets. Soon he was hopelessly lost.

"I'm sorry, man," Ramone said out loud. He was thinking about how disappointed Lightning was going to be when they lost the race. Then, a miracle! Ramone glanced down a long street – and saw Brakeaway Tunnel in the distance. He hit the gas. "Hang on, Lightning," he cried. "I'm coming!"

Suddenly Chick came zooming up next to Ramone and pushed him against a warehouse. Ramone had nowhere to go but up the ramp to the building's loading dock. There he launched himself off.

"I love to drive," shouted Ramone. "But when you're short on time, flying is the only way to go!"

Chick had accidentally helped Ramone get even closer to the relay point!

Ramone floored it while Chick blasted out of the side street. Both cars reached Brakeaway Tunnel and tagged their partners at exactly the same time!

Lightning was a blur as he entered the tunnel just before Stinger. Seconds later – thanks to Chick – the lights went out. Lightning had to slow down. Without headlights, he couldn't see a thing. Then his eyes adjusted. His new paint job was casting a glow inside the tunnel! "Thank you, Ramone!" Lightning cried.

Stinger was on Lightning's tail as they exited the tunnel. Then he accelerated and rammed into his opponent. Lightning skidded into a big pothole – and couldn't get out!

"Lucky hit!" Lightning yelled. "I'd like to see you do that again!"

BAM! Stinger hit Lightning so hard that he lurched right out of the hole.

"Thanks!" called Lightning as he took the lead once again. "I couldn't have done it without you!"

Chick was watching from the sidelines as Stinger was losing ground. "I don't care what you have to do – just cross that finish line first!" he yelled.

Stinger knew what that meant. He left the road and took a short cut through a parking lot.

POP! POP! POP! POP! All four of his tyres went flat!

Meanwhile, Lightning crossed the finish line to the cheers of his fans. "Ka-chow!" he exclaimed as he posed for the cameras. "The best racing school in the world wins again!"

A little while later, Lightning and Ramone proudly accepted their Silver Tailfin Trophy. "Lightning," said a reporter, "do you have any words of advice for Chick and Stinger?" "Yeah," said Lightning. "Racing the wrong way is never the right thing to do!"

The End

THE STORY OF THE FILM

Finn McMissile, a British secret agent had slipped onto an oil derrick. He was spying on a spectacled criminal named Professor Z.

Finn hid in the rafters and took photos of a TV camera. He also saw another secret agent who had been crushed into scrap metal!

Back in Radiator Springs, race car Lightning McQueen was at the Wheel Well Restaurant. Miles Axlerod, a former oil tycoon and Francesco Bernoulli, an Italian race car were on TV. Axlerod was hosting an international race called the World Grand Prix to introduce his new alternative fuel, Allinol. Lightning agreed to join the race.

Lightning and his pit crew soon arrived in Tokyo for the first race. Mater embarrassed Lightning at the welcome party. He even leaked oil beside Axlerod.

Mater raced off to the bathroom. Inside the automated cubicle, he got poked, prodded and splashed with water!

135

While Mater was in the cubicle, two members of Professor Z's crew, Grem and Acer, roughed up American Agent Rod "Torque" Redline. When Mater came out of the cubicle, Torque secretly stuck a device underneath Mater.

The following day at the racetrack, Finn and his fellow agent Holley Shiftwell kept a close eye on Mater. They thought he was a secret agent, too!

Nearby, Grem and Acer aimed the TV camera at a race car. The camera was a weapon! Seconds later, the car's engine exploded. Some thought Allinol was to blame.

Professor Z's gang then went after Mater in the pits. They wanted the device that the American agent had planted on him.

Just as the bad cars were closing in on Mater, Finn rushed in to the rescue. Mater thought he was watching a karate demonstration!

Since Mater was distracted, he gave Lightning bad racing tips. Lightning ended up losing the race to Francesco!

Lightning blamed Mater. "I lost the race because of you!" he exclaimed.

Mater felt so terrible he decided to go back home. But Finn and Holley whisked him off on a spy mission instead.

Holley removed the planted device from Mater and found a photo of a mysterious, gas-guzzling engine. Mater noticed it had Whitworth bolts, which were very difficult to unscrew.

Meanwhile, Lightning and his team were just outside Porto Corsa, Italy visiting Luigi and Guido's hometown. Lightning talked to Luigi's Uncle Topolino about his fight with Mater.

"Everybody fights now and then, especially best friends," said Uncle Topolino. "But you gotta make up fast."

Holley, Finn and Mater were also on their way to Porto Corsa. Mater had told them the mysterious engine belonged to a Lemon – a car that didn't work right. They soon found out that a secret meeting of Lemons was being held in Porto Corsa. Holley disguised Mater as one of the Lemons' tow trucks so he could sneak into the meeting. She also gave him lots of spy gadgets!

Mater was soon in a room with Professor Z and all the Lemons. Then their "Big Boss", whose identity was hidden, appeared on a TV screen. He told the Lemons that once Allinol was proven dangerous, all cars would go back to using gasoline. Then the Lemons, who owned most of the world's oil, would become wealthy and powerful.

Outside, the second race had begun. Grem and Acer were on a nearby tower with the camera. They aimed it at the race car from Brazil. Her engine suddenly exploded! Finn raced to the tower to stop Grem and Acer – but a helicopter captured him with a giant magnet!

Back at the race, Lightning crossed the finish line first! He then announced that he would still be using Allinol in the final World Grand Prix race in London. The Big Boss heard this and gave the order to get rid of Lightning. Mater used his parachute to escape from the meeting. But before he could warn Lightning, Mater was kidnapped by the Lemons. They had captured Holley, too!

Finn, Holley and Mater were tied up inside the clockworks of Big Bentley in London. Mater finally convinced Finn and Holley that he wasn't a spy.

After the final race began, Grem and Acer told Mater they had planted a bomb inside Lightning's pit. As soon as the Lemons left, Mater escaped, racing to save his best friend.

Minutes later, Holley and Finn escaped, too. They soon discovered the Lemons had actually planted the bomb on Mater! Finn radioed the tow truck to tell him, but Mater was already in the pits.

"Stay away from me!" Mater warned Lightning.

But Lightning still raced forwards to see his best friend!

Meanwhile, Professor Z tried to escape on a combat ship, but Finn stopped him. He tied the Professor up in cables and brought him to Holley, Mater and Lightning. Then Guido tried to remove the bomb on Mater, but he couldn't unscrew the bolts. Suddenly, everything made sense to Mater. He knew who the Big Boss was!

Mater flew with Lightning to Buckingham Palace. Mater told everyone that Axlerod was the Big Boss! Mater figured it out because the bolts on the bomb were the same Whitworth bolts from the old British engine in the photo. The engine belonged to Axlerod. He was the biggest Lemon of all. Axlerod deactivated the bomb and everyone was saved.

The Queen thanked Mater by making him a knight!

Not long after Lightning got back home, he decided to hold his own "Radiator Springs Grand Prix."

He invited all the international race cars. The whole town turned out for the race.

Finn and Holley showed up, too. They had come to invite
Mater on their next mission. Mater politely turned them down. But
he did take his spy gadgets for one last spin. Mater activated his
rockets and blasted off down the racetrack, right beside his best friend.

The End

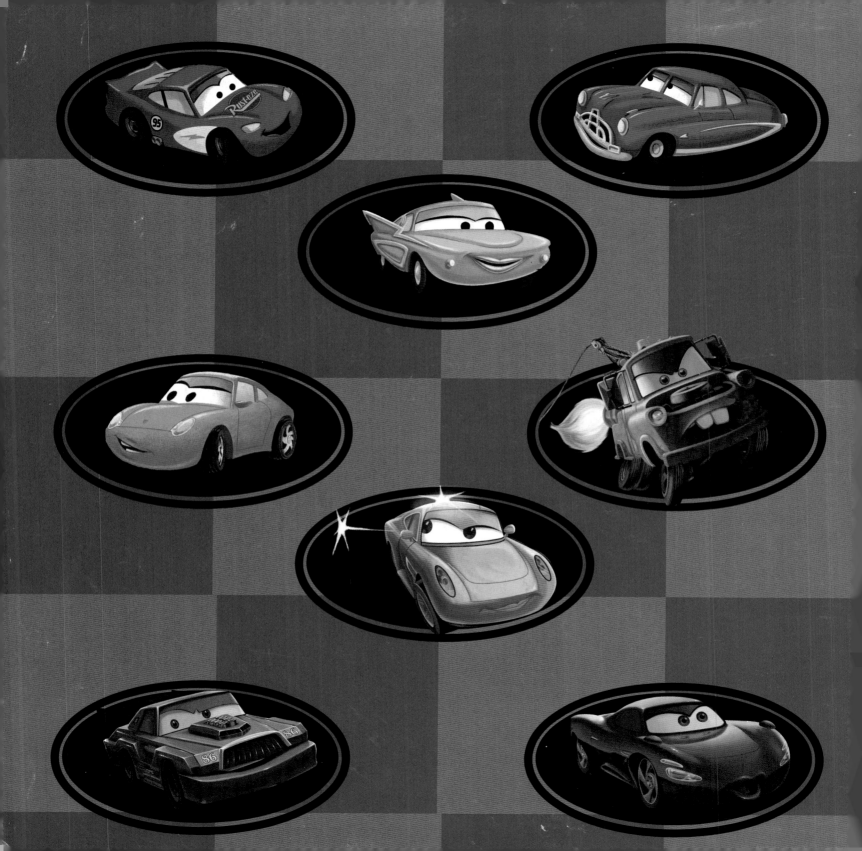